JOAN W. BLOS

Martin's Hats

ILLUSTRATED BY MARC SIMONT

WILLIAM MORROW AND COMPANY

For Betty Miles

10 9 8 7 6 5 4 3

Library of Congress Cataloging in Publication Data
Blos, Joan W.   Martin's Hats.
Summary: A variety of hats afford Martin many adventures. [1. Hats—
Fiction. 2. Play—Fiction] I. Simont, Marc, ill. II. title.
PZ7.B6237Mar 1984   [E]   83-13389
ISBN 0-688-02027-5
ISBN 0-688-02033-X (lib. bdg.)

Martin's explorer hat was the kind
used by real explorers
when going to far-off places.
Martin put on his hat
and went upstairs in his house.

He squeezed into caves
dark as under the bed,

and climbed the lesser mountains.
He was surprised to see
who lived up there.
It was his good luck
that a party hat was near.
Martin put on the party hat
and joined them at their party.

At the end of the party
someone told…

about a train that could not go
for want of an engineer.

Martin put on his engineer's cap,
fired up the ancient machine,
got her ready and told his conductor,
"We'll be on time to Chicago!"
"All aboard," yelled the conductor.

"The *American Flyer* is now ready for departure.
Stopping at Albany, Troy, Schenectady,
Mt. Albans, Ann Arbor, Point of the Pines,
Cincinnati, Detroit, and Chicago."
The passengers were delighted
and responded with a cheer.

Arriving in Chicago
many were hungry.
Martin greeted them happily
and served them an excellent meal.

There was, in Chicago, a great deal to do
as in any big city.
In rapid order Martin
directed the traffic,
        delivered the mail,
                and put out a fire.

Then he welded a girder.
From the
height
of the
skeleton
building
Martin could see broad fields.

It was just time
to harvest the hay,

and to bring in the corn
for the cattle.

A farmer's day ends early.
Home from the fields
Martin hung up his hat,
washed up,
and ate his dinner.

Just as darkness reached the sky
Martin reached his room.

A special hat was waiting.
"Just the thing for a nightcap," he said,

and wore it
while going
to sleep.
That's all, and it's—
The End

DATE DUE

MAR 12 2019	
APR 22 2019	
4/17/2019	

PRINTED IN U.S.A.